The Lion Who Ate EVERYTHING

Tobias Hill

illustrated by Michael Foreman

WALKER BOOKS
AND SUBSIDIARIES
LONDON • BOSTON • SYDNEY • AUCKLAND

The Lion Who Ate EVERYTHING

For Dorothy, Mabel and Jess – T.H.

For Ben Norland – M.F.

First published 2008 by Walker Books Ltd, 87 Vauxhall Walk, London SE11 5HJ

2 4 6 8 10 9 7 5 3 1

This book has been typeset in Monotype Bembo and Franklin Gothic Condensed

Printed in China

British Library Cataloguing in Publication Data:

a catalogue record for this book is available from the British Library

ISBN 978-1-4063-0859-4

www.walkerbooks.co.uk

ONCE there was a lion who loved to eat. Everyone likes eating, but the lion loved it. Some people called it greedy, but the lion just smiled. "Greed," it purred, "is in my nature."

That lion was so greedy it would eat anything. It ate fast food and snack food and junk food and junk. It ate rusty cans and water mains and bits of fluff and subway trains and ceiling fans – and other stuff.

You see? When it got greedy, the lion ate anything.

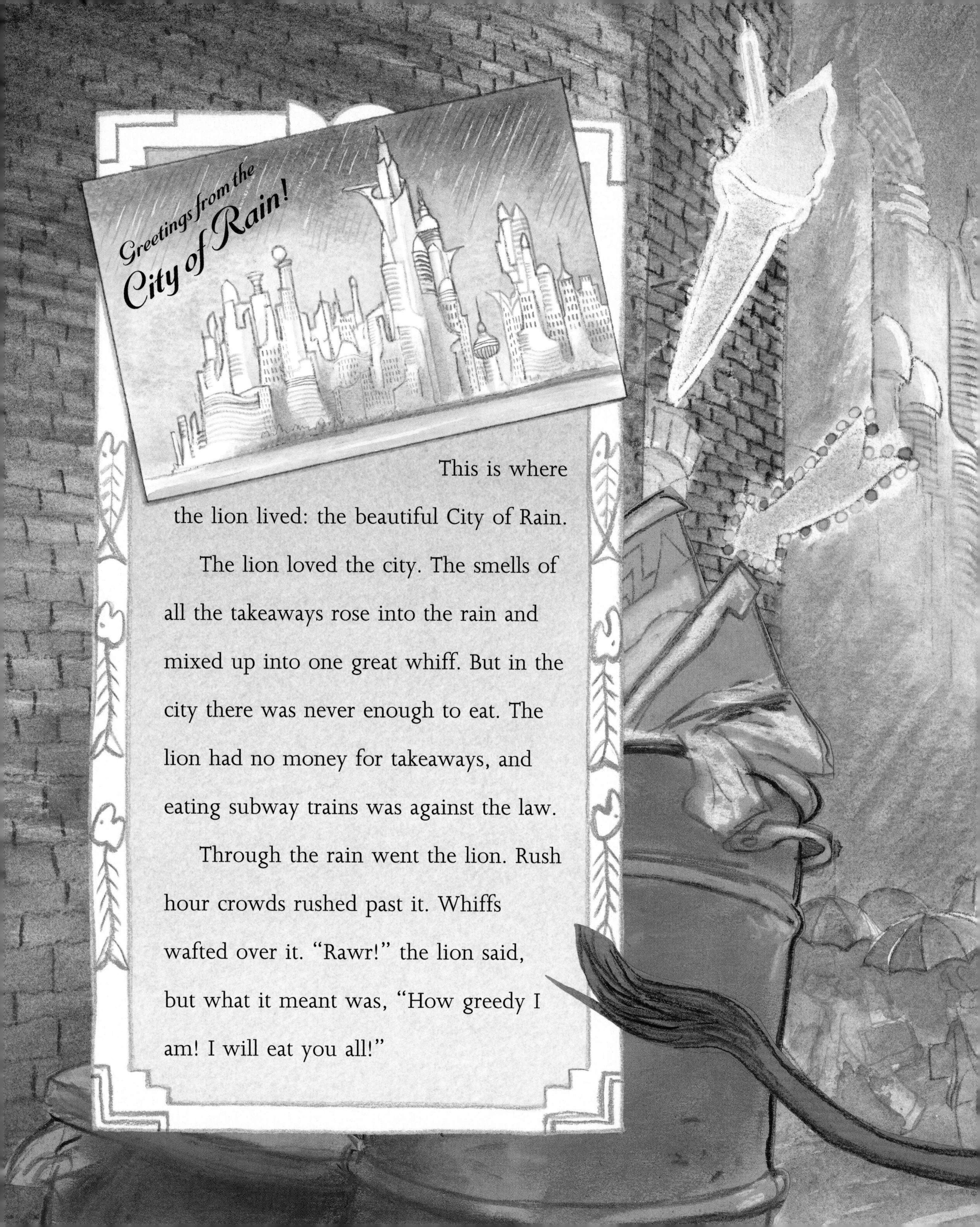

This is where the lion lived: the beautiful City of Rain.

The lion loved the city. The smells of all the takeaways rose into the rain and mixed up into one great whiff. But in the city there was never enough to eat. The lion had no money for takeaways, and eating subway trains was against the law.

Through the rain went the lion. Rush hour crowds rushed past it. Whiffs wafted over it. "Rawr!" the lion said, but what it meant was, "How greedy I am! I will eat you all!"

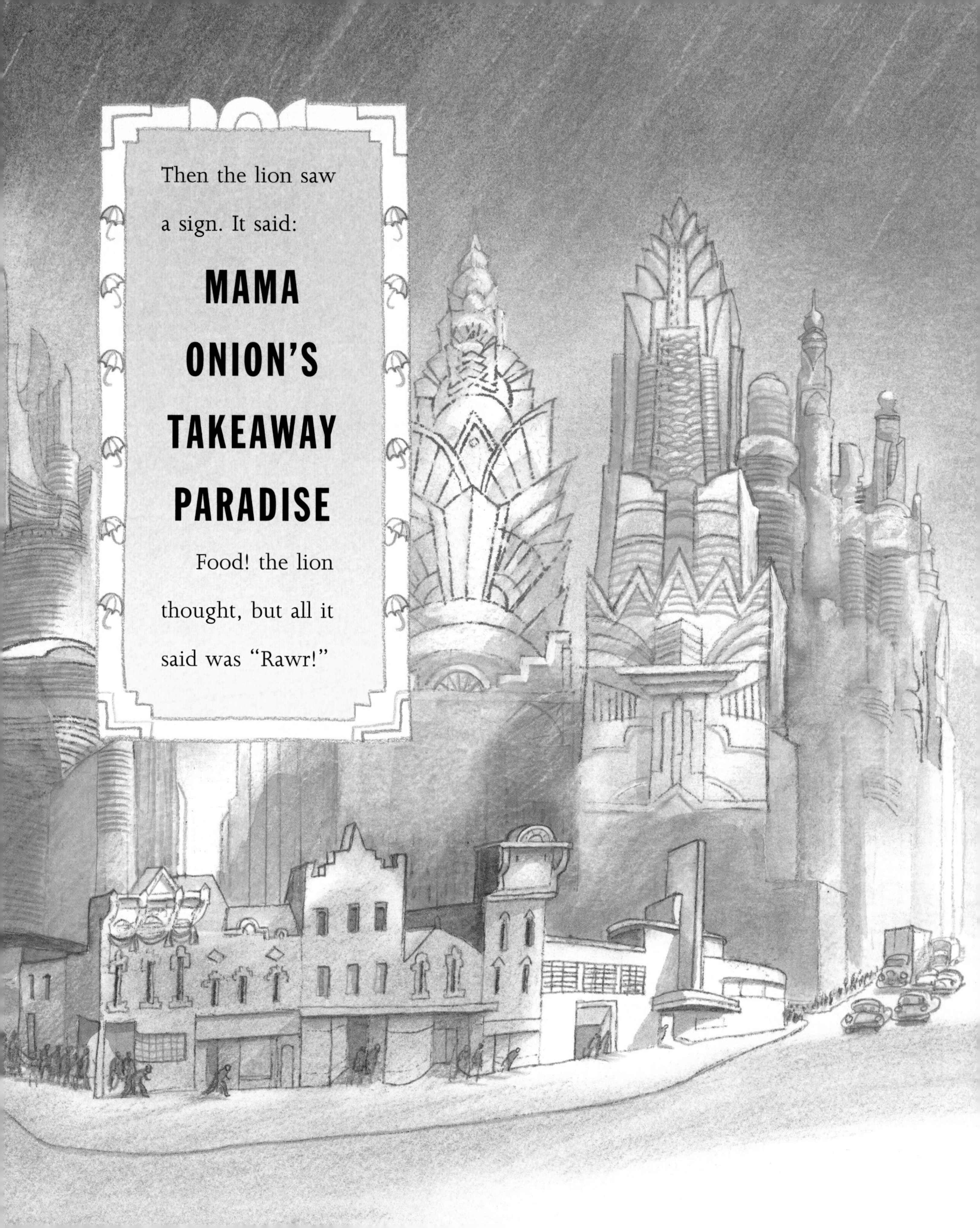
Then the lion saw
a sign. It said:
MAMA
ONION'S
TAKEAWAY
PARADISE
Food! the lion
thought, but all it
said was "Rawr!"

MAMA ONIONS
EATS
TAKE AWAY
DINER

Mama Onion was doing the crossword. Some people might have been alarmed to find a lion at the door. Not Mama Onion.

"Well!" said Mama Onion, "if it ain't that lion I heard about. They say you're the greediest thing in the whole city. Is that right?"

"Rawr!" said the lion.

"That's no good!" Mama Onion said. "Hunger is a fine thing, but you shouldn't get greedy or one day you'll be sorry. Lucky for you that you found me. Onion's my name, cooking's my game. I'll teach you how to eat just enough. What do they call you?"

"Lion," said the lion.

"That's no kind of name!"

She put down her crossword and picked up her glasses. "You've got nice eyes. You need a nice name. I'll call you Leo. Now then, Leo – it's feeding time."

And so saying, she reached under her counter and lifted out...

"The Great Dane Hot Dog! One should do – two would be greedy."

The whiff of onions filled the shop – Mmm! – but would any hot dog be enough for a lion? It closed its eyes and –

SCHLUPP!

– breathed in; and in a lick of mustard, the hot dog was gone.

"Ho!" said Mama Onion. "Looks like the Great Dane ain't quite enough." And she reached down again and heaved out…

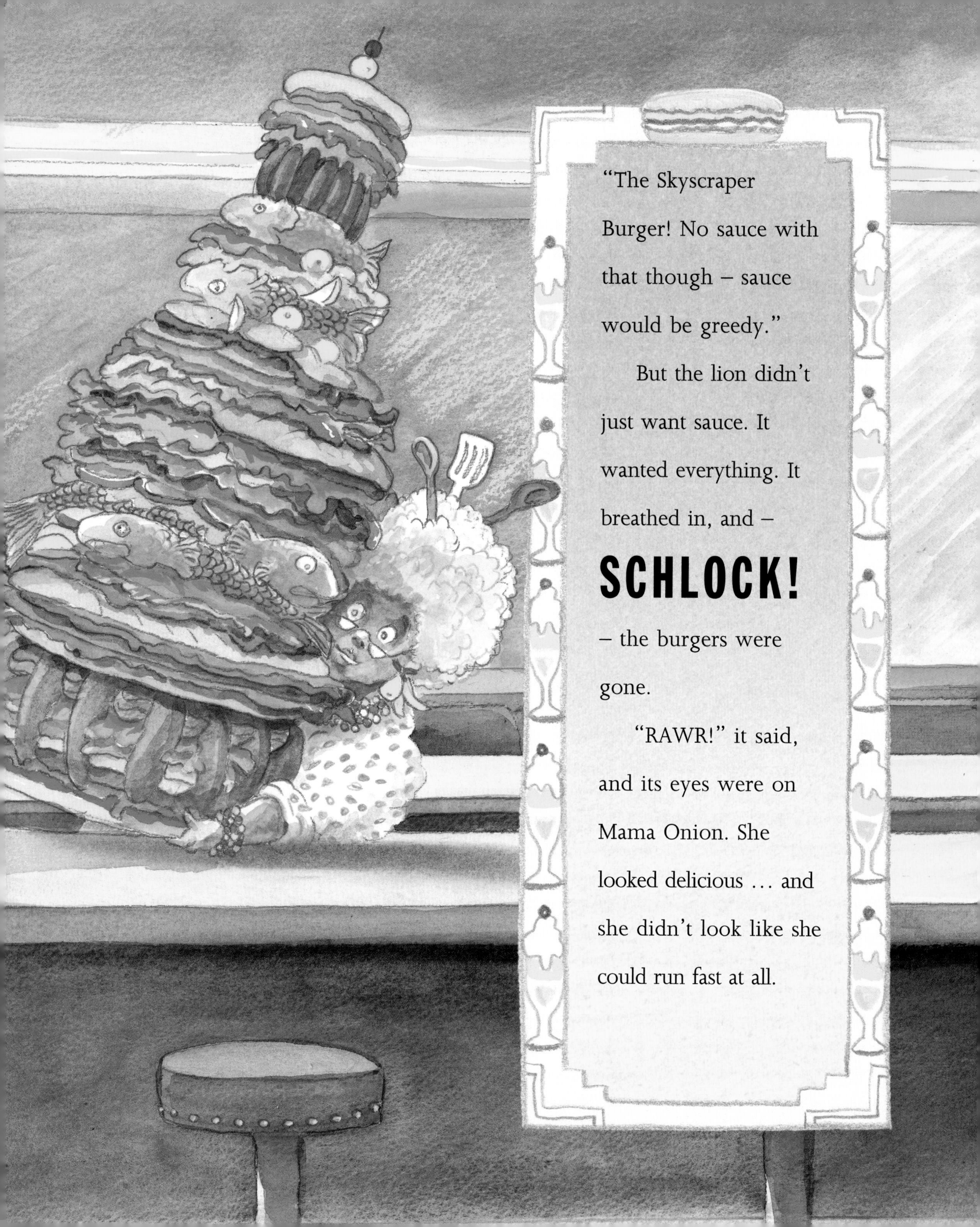

"The Skyscraper Burger! No sauce with that though – sauce would be greedy."

But the lion didn't just want sauce. It wanted everything. It breathed in, and –

SCHLOCK!

– the burgers were gone.

"RAWR!" it said, and its eyes were on Mama Onion. She looked delicious ... and she didn't look like she could run fast at all.

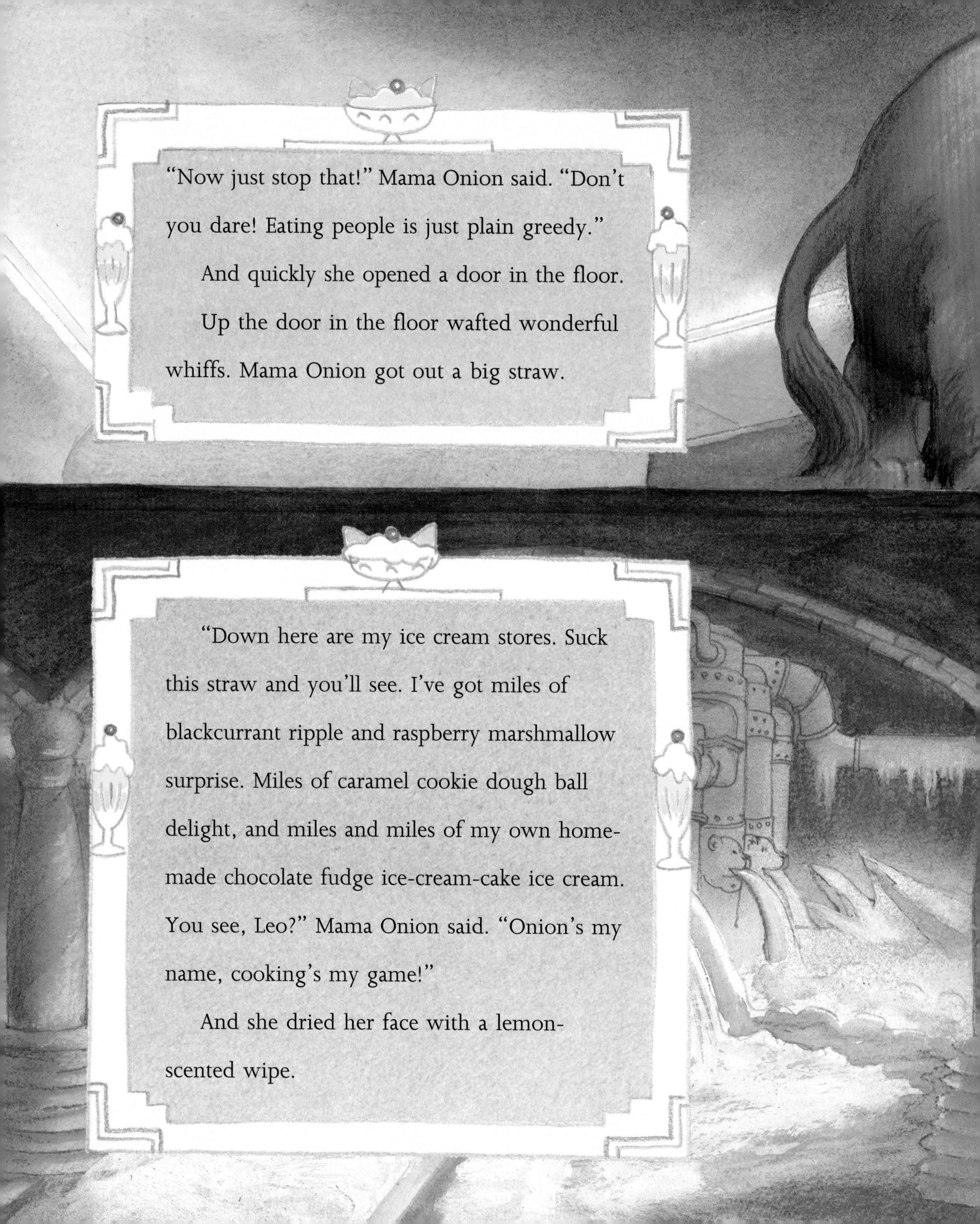

"Now just stop that!" Mama Onion said. "Don't you dare! Eating people is just plain greedy."

And quickly she opened a door in the floor.

Up the door in the floor wafted wonderful whiffs. Mama Onion got out a big straw.

"Down here are my ice cream stores. Suck this straw and you'll see. I've got miles of blackcurrant ripple and raspberry marshmallow surprise. Miles of caramel cookie dough ball delight, and miles and miles of my own home-made chocolate fudge ice-cream-cake ice cream. You see, Leo?" Mama Onion said. "Onion's my name, cooking's my game!"

And she dried her face with a lemon-scented wipe.

The lion took the straw and sucked. First came the ice-cream-cake ice cream. Then came the blackcurrant ripple. One by one the ice creams went into the lion. Bit by bit the lion got bigger.

A distant rumbling began. Mama Onion looked down. "It ain't possible!" she said. The rumbling was getting louder. Then it stopped with two sounds. One went like this:

THHHWOOO-OO-IPP

– and the other went like this:

RONCH!

"It's the end of the ice cream!" Mama Onion screamed, and she was right. The ice cream had ended; and the lion had gone through the roof.

Mama Onion grabbed her cookbook and ran.

EATS
AY
DINER

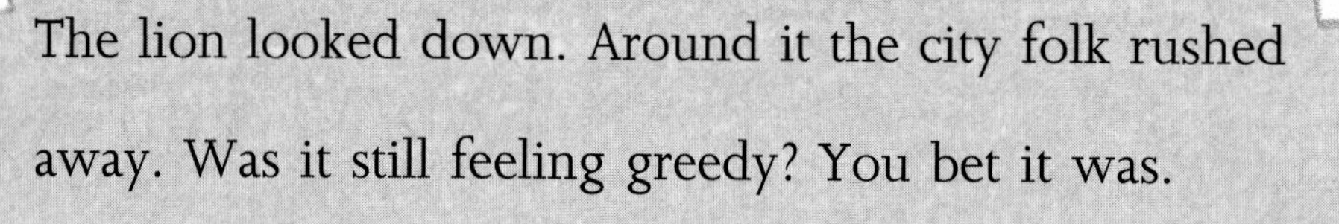

The lion looked down. Around it the city folk rushed away. Was it still feeling greedy? You bet it was.

Mmm, city folks … the lion would have eaten them, but they weren't enough. It was as a big as a house, and so was its greed.

Down the road came a fire engine. The lion breathed in, and

FLOOOOP!

and

CRUNCH!

and it was gone. But that wasn't enough either. Greed, the lion thought, is in my nature. But it didn't say that. All it could say was "RAWRRR!" – and even that was hard with its mouth full.

It could see the city all around. It could smell the great whiff of it. Its stomach rumbled, and when it roared, aeroplanes turned back on their ways to Alaska and Zanzibar.

Street by street, it began to eat the city. It tasted like a pizza with every topping on the menu. It went on eating for a long time. Then it
GLUPPED,
but only once.

The lion opened its eyes.

The city was gone. There was nothing left but grass.

Far away it could see Mama Onion, still running.

Its eyes fell on the curve of the world. It was green and soft under its claws. It smelled as fresh as an apple.

The lion opened its mouth and ...

...sighed.

That sigh shook the earth. When Mama Onion heard it she walked back to the lion.

"Still feeling greedy?" she said, but the lion shook its head.

"Tired, I bet."

But the lion shook its head again.

What was it Mama Onion had said? You shouldn't get greedy, or one day you'll be sorry. And now that day had come.

The lion felt sorry the city was gone. It missed the people and the whiffs. Nothing was left except the rain.

"Don't tell me you're sorry?"

But it was.

"Well," Mama Onion said, "I won't say I told you so."

Tears rolled down the lion's face. Mama Onion wiped them away. "Looks like being sorry is in your nature."

"What use is sorry?" the lion growled. "The beautiful City of Rain is gone. And what will happen next time? Greed is in my nature."

"Bah!" said Mama Onion. "Humbug! Greed ain't natural. Greed isn't in your nature. You just get mighty hungry, that's all. And I know what to do about hunger... I'll teach you to cook! Onion's my name, cooking's my game. A cook never goes hungry. You won't want to eat everything when you can make yourself anything. What do you say? Can I teach you?"

"Cooking..." purred the lion. "I think it might be in my nature."

It lay down by Mama Onion and fell asleep. "Rawr!" it said, but it was snoring, not roaring.

And meanwhile Mama Onion opened her cookbook,

and turned to Breakfast.

Lion and Onions
Restaurant
OPENING SOON!